# Color my Christmas

## Natalie-Nicole Bates

# EXCERPT FROM COLOR MY CHRISTMAS

She walked to the window and turned back to him. "Come here, Timothy, I want to show you something."

He got up from the couch, quite curious. It was dark outside now, and the main street below was still in full swing. People walked up and down the street. Each store was brightly lit, and gaily decorated in festive colors.

"Look at that, Timothy." She stood so close, he could hear her gentle breath, and feel the heat from her body. "This is Christmas. This is life."

He placed his hand on the icy window. Perhaps it was time to let go of what he couldn't change, and embrace what was still real. If he was strong enough to do it. He stole a glance at Meggie who stared with delight at the hustle and bustle below. Maybe with this woman by his side, he could very well pull himself back from the depths of hell and rejoin the living.

*She will be easy to spot...she's so unusual. In the most spectacular way. You're going to fall in love with her*!

These were his mother's words.

*Yeah, right.*

He'd made it more than thirty years without really falling in love. Sure, he'd been infatuated from time to time, but not real, full-blown love. He seriously doubted it would ever happen for him. Besides, he was at the community center for a purpose—not to find a wife, and certainly not because he wanted to be here at the Lillian Lane Community Center, also known as the place his life changed forever, and not for the better.

He was here to see Meggie Marie— her real name, but whether it was her first and last name, or simply a first and middle name, surname unknown, Timothy didn't know. Meggie Marie was his last chance to heal.

The biting early December wind whipped furiously around his face. He huddled into his jacket, and made his way up the few concrete steps to the entrance. As he reached for the handle of the door, he stopped suddenly, and caught sight of the jagged scar. Reaching into his pocket, he pulled out a pair of wool gloves and slid them on. Crazy to put gloves on entering a building, but he had reasons. He didn't want people staring at his hand, and didn't want to scare any kids who might catch a glimpse of it.

A blast of welcoming warm air greeted him inside, as well as the smell of freshly baked cookies.

There were a lot of classes every afternoon, and with Christmas just a few short weeks away, likely an uptake in people taking a last minute baking or craft class.

The place was decorated to the maximum for Christmas. Strings of twinkling lights hung over windows, a tree full of what looked like handmade ornaments, stood in a corner, and Christmas artwork from scribbles to some fairly decent paintings, covered the walls. Too bad he couldn't get into the Christmas spirit.

Timothy walked to the reception desk. The woman behind it looked up from the computer screen.

"I'm looking for Meggie Marie. I was told she might be here this afternoon."

"Oh, perfect timing." The woman smiled, and turned back toward one of the open doors. "Her little students should be just about finished for the day." As she said the words, a line of children emerged. They were different ages, from about six to nine, he guessed. Both boys and girls.

"Thank you."

Timothy waited outside the classroom until the last student scampered out into her mother's waiting arms. To be polite, he knocked on the doorframe of the classroom, but did not enter uninvited. To his dismay, when he poked his head inside, the room appeared deserted. Maybe he'd missed Meggie Marie altogether. Perhaps she'd slipped out some back door. He grumbled under his breath. What a complete waste of time.

Just when he turned to leave, a voice called out behind him. A lovely, lilting voice.

"Can I help you?"

He turned back quickly. His mother had been right! He knew her in an instant, without as much as an introduction: Meggie Marie, with bright, festive red hair adorned with a headband of large green roses that would seem ostentatious on almost any other woman. Yet she carried it off magnificently. She wore a dress of tie-dye green that fell to her knees. She was petite, but curvy with porcelain skin and beautiful red lips that reminded him of a perfect doll. When she smiled, she just…shone. She wasn't the kind of woman that usually attracted him, but she was something special, and he didn't even know her. He'd never been hit so fast, or so hard before.

Finally, he remembered why he was there, and found his voice before she could think he was some random psycho off the street. "I'm Timothy Martin, Alma's son."

A light of recognition flashed in her brilliant brown eyes. "Oh yes!" she gushed. "It's so nice to meet you." She extended her hand.

For a moment, he stared at her outstretched hand, but then clasped it gently with her gloved one. For a few seconds, everything was quiet between them, to the point of almost uncomfortable. Timothy knew he'd better get to the reason he was there, and get there fast.

"My mother tells me you have a way of dealing with hopeless cases. That you actually got a woman at the assisted living community to write her name again after a severe stroke. Can you show me how you did that?"

She let out a bit of a sigh and pressed her lips together. "I know you're a doctor, Timothy, your mother mentioned that. I'm sure you understand that what I do can't really be taught. I sort of feel my way through a treatment, depending on the client's circumstances. Also, I'm not always successful. You are a medical professional, and what I provide is more alternative healing."

It dawned on him that she thought he was there to learn her methods, to perhaps steal any secrets she possessed in healing. She didn't realize he was there for her help, that she was his last chance.

"Actually…" His voice trailed off and he cleared his throat. "I need treatment." After he spoke the truth, a group of laughing women passed by the open door, and his cheeks heated, even though he knew the women weren't laughing at him. "Is there somewhere quiet we can talk?"

She smiled, and his troubled soul calmed just a bit. "Sure, let me clean up and put away my students' gingerbread houses. The community center will be closing soon, so if you could help, that would be marvelous."

*Marvelous*. It was a word he seldom heard from anyone. Yet coming from her lips, it sounded...*marvelous*. He nearly laughed out loud. Laughing was something he didn't do much of anymore. He watched as she went about putting the partially constructed gingerbread houses on to a shelf, and then followed her lead. Some of the houses looked like they were out of a horror movie, or barely survived a tornado. It was more Halloween than Christmas. Meggie looked at them with such admiration and love all the same.

When they finished, he helped her into her red coat with a little Christmas wreath broach attached at the lapel with tiny, flashing red and green lights.

"So, is your name really Meggie Marie?"

Her dark brows drew together as she lifted her handbag. "Of course. Why would you ask that?"

"I didn't know if Marie was your surname, middle name, or what have you."

"Oh." She paused and pursed her lips. "Meggie is my first name, Marie is my surname."

"Is that short for Margaret?" he asked as he followed her from the classroom.

She stopped and turned off the overhead lighting, before she continued out the door. When they reached the lobby, she turned back to him. "Meghan, not Margaret. Just call me Meggie."

He didn't know why, but he liked this woman. If she liked being called Meggie, that was just fine with him, as long as he got to spend more time with this wonderfully different woman.

Meggie had a secret. She knew all about Dr. Timothy Martin, and his circumstances. She'd even known he was coming to see her. Alma Martin, Timothy's mother, told her all about him, and the unfortunate happening in his life a year or so earlier. Alma made Meggie promise not to let on that she was well aware of his situation, and that her son was a proud man, who now felt helpless. She felt for sure he wouldn't tell Meggie everything. Because she considered Alma a friend, and a devoted mother to her son, but mostly because she really thought she could help Timothy, she reluctantly agreed to keep quiet—for now. Every time she thought of withholding the truth from Timothy, it caused a knot in her stomach.

Well, he would come into her life and out again in a few days, maybe a few weeks, and probably would be none the wiser that his mother meddled in his personal life, and she went along with the rouse. If it did him any good, maybe the rouse would be worth it. Maybe.

The late afternoon sky was beginning to darken, and a flurry of snowflakes began to fall as they turned into the Cozy Corner Café for a chat. Meggie draped her coat over a chair, and took a seat at the back of the café.

"I love this place, especially all the Christmas decorations, and with that roaring fire behind us, it's even lovelier." She rubbed her cold hands together to warm them.

Timothy looked around at all of the twinkling Christmas lights and holiday décor, and slipped into the chair across from her. "It's nice"—his voice trailed off—"if you're into the Christmas sort of thing."

Meggie knew just from the inflection in his voice, the way his posture stooped, and the fact he still wore gloves indoors, Timothy Martin was a very sad man who felt his world was broken. Sometimes feelings and emotions became starker, more acute at the holidays. Maybe she could help him put his life back together again. It might not be the same, but perhaps it could be just as fulfilling, and hopefully even more so. She made a bit of small talk with him while they waited for their order. She didn't want to start a serious discussion only to be interrupted.

A few minutes passed, and their coffee and blueberry spice muffins were delivered to the table. As she used a knife to cut her muffin into pieces, she casually spoke. "So, Timothy, how is it I can help you?"

"Well, I…um…" he stammered, and raked a hand through his light hair. "I'm not sure if my mother mentioned to you, I had a rather unfortunate incident last year at the medical clinic at the community center?"

This was hard for him, she knew, especially when she looked into his blue eyes. So much emotion, and none of it positive.

Every fiber of her being told her to come clean, tell him she knew everything. If he got up and left, then he wasn't ready to accept help, or the truth about his condition. Still, all she managed to say was, "She did mention to me you were assaulted trying to break up a fight."

"I have a lot of nerve damage in my left hand." He wrung his gloved hands together for emphasis.

"Unfortunately for me, I'm left-handed, and I am…I *was* a surgeon, so you can see my predicament."

She stirred cream into her coffee. They were both left-handed. One small point in common. "I imagine you've exhausted everything medically possible before coming to see me?"

"Well, yes, but that doesn't mean your service is any less valuable."

"Believe me, Timothy, I'm not offended. People usually resort to seeing me when they've exercised every other option." She fixed her brown eyes to his blue. "That is why I tell everyone who comes to me that I'm not a miracle worker."

He smiled, and to Meggie, he suddenly looked ten years younger.

"My mother wouldn't agree with that. She believes you *are* a miracle. She says just being around you makes people feel better. I can't thank you enough for helping her out. After her surgery, she was so depressed. She fell in love with your craft and baking classes, and just being around you."

"Oh, that's so sweet. Your mother is such a gem."

"I do believe you are blushing, Meggie," he teased.

She touched her cheeks. She really wasn't embarrassed, more amused. "It must be the December cold on my pale skin."

"Hmm, maybe so."

Now she needed to ask a difficult question. "Could you take off your gloves and let me see your hand?"

Immediately, he looked around as though about to reveal some top secret plans and wanted no one nearby to eavesdrop. He slipped off his gloves and laid them on the table. He reached across the table, palm up, and she saw the huge jagged scar that crisscrossed his palm. She didn't as much as flinch, took his larger hand into her smaller one, and ran her thumb over the scars. She turned his hand over and was shocked to see the back of his hand and fingers were also badly scarred.

"A lot of surgery, huh?" She looked up at him.

"A lot of damage, followed by surgery, and physical therapy that did nothing to help."

She doubted he had no relief at all, but just looking at his hand, she knew she could not perform some Christmas miracle. She hated to say never, but realistically, she knew the truth. Taking both of his hands into hers, she took him through a few tests to gauge his strength, muscle tone, and limitations. He squeezed both of her hands, and she was pleased to see he still had almost equal strength. He pushed her outstretched palms away with his palms, and then pulled her taut fingers toward him. For the amount of damage he suffered, he was surprisingly agile, but when she handed him a pen and a pad of paper and asked him to write his name and her name, the truth was glaring. He could barely write his own name, let alone hers. He was never going to perform surgery again, she confirmed in her own mind.

He pushed the pad and pen across the table. "I'm sorry about that, it doesn't look like it's been written by a college-educated human."

Before he could pull his hand back, she placed hers on top of his. "Hey, Timothy, we're going to work on it, okay? And after some time, we'll see if there is any improvement. You know there are so many things you can do with your medical degree besides surgery."

Natalie-Nicole Bates

He rolled his blue eyes as though he'd heard this tiresome lecture time and time again.

"Medical research, general practice, a change of specialty such as hematology, where you wouldn't be required to use a scalpel. When one door closes—"

He waved her off. "Yeah, yeah, another one opens and all that nonsense."

"No," she corrected him. "For you, one door may have closed, but the number of doors that can open for you are almost unlimited. We just have to find the right door."

He shrugged, but she ignored it. This was part of the grieving process, and the death he experienced, at least on the surface, was his career. He couldn't yet see beyond that closed door.

That was where she stepped in.

24

"Timothy, do you want my help, or don't you?" she asked him blatantly.

"Yeah, I guess so," he replied flatly.

So much for a solid commitment.

"I'll take that as a yes. When do you want to begin?"

"Good grief, Meggie, I thought I was in pretty good shape until I walked up all those metal steps."

She smiled at the first words that greeted her the next afternoon at her apartment, which was situated above a busy bakery in the middle of town. She didn't have an office, and preferred to do the majority of her work from a clinical environment. A few hours a week at the senior center, another six hours at the local hospital's rehab unit, two assisted living facilities. It kept her busy and only enough time to take on one or two private clients a year. With it being Christmas season she hoped to take a break for a few weeks, but she couldn't say no to Timothy's mother. It seemed paramount to her that her son enjoy Christmas, and look forward to a bright, happy new year. Neither of which she could promise or provide. She didn't mind offering hope, but she would never offer false hope no matter what the situation.

"I love living here. It's only me, and every morning I wake to the smell of fresh bread baking downstairs."

"I don't know if bread is worth walking those stairs day in and day out." He leaned against the door and continued to breathe hard.

"You'll get used to it."

"Or, you could come to my place." He raised a brow. "No steps, and I will pick you up and drive you home, if you'd like."

It didn't really matter where they worked as long as they had privacy. She didn't drive, but instead utilized public transportation, and the occasional luxury of a taxi. If Timothy was more comfortable in his own surroundings, she was fine with that as long as he was willing to drive.

"We could arrange that, I suppose. Maybe alternate. But since you're here, let's get started. Coffee or tea?"

"Coffee, please," he answered as he took off his jacket and hung it on an empty hook near the door.

ked into the kitchenette, and turned on

e. As the water heated, she spooned

coffee crystals into a mug.

"Why don't you take a seat at the table? I'll be there in a jiff."

"A jiff? I like the way you talk, Meggie— quirky—and the way you dress. I've never known a woman who could pull off tie-dye dresses and actually look amazing in them...not to mention those fancy headbands you wear."

There was something about the guy, but she couldn't put a finger on exactly what it was that made her feel butterflies in her stomach when they talked. Sure, he was handsome and smart, but also her client, and in the throes of accepting a life-altering change. She poured boiling water over the coffee crystals, and then placed the coffee mug on a coaster beside him.

Immediately, he moved the coaster to his right side and lifted it with his right hand.

"Left hand, please. I know it's easier to just use your off hand, but you need to keep the left hand as functional as possible.

He grimaced. "So, the lessons begin already?"

"Look Timothy, I know you don't want to be here. I know you're angry at everyone in this world for what happened to your hand. I also know because I'm left-handed, too, that sometimes the world doesn't adapt to that, and you have to adapt to it by using your right hand for certain things. I'm just asking you to give it a try, okay?"

Behind his eyes she could almost see his mind processing what she asked of him. Finally, he nodded a few times. "Okay, I'll try. Also, I hope you don't think

I'm being snippy with you. I truly appreciate what you're doing for me."

"Don't worry about that"—she turned on a smile—"I've been yelled at, had things thrown at me, you name it. When people meet me, or interact with me, most of the time it's because something traumatic happened in their lives. I'm the convenient thing to lash out at."

"You're not a thing. My mother tells me you are an absolute doll, and that you are sweet and loving, and dedicated."

There was that sweet talk again that could melt her into a puddle.

"I just love your mother. She has become a good friend to me, and to see the leaps and bounds she's made since her surgery, well, that's just so fulfilling."

Now it was time to get back to therapy.

"I think that the most effective therapy for you is coloring therapy."

"What's that?" he asked suspiciously.

She reached for the packet she'd prepared for him that morning.

"It's exactly what it says." She unloaded an adult coloring book from the blue canvas tote bag. "Colored pencils, crayons, and markers...but I don't think you're ready for markers just yet." When she looked at him, he was actually scowling, and his arms were crossed over his chest. She laughed out loud, even though she knew it was totally inappropriate. Still, the look on his face was priceless.

"Laugh if you must, Meggie, but I draw the line at children's activities. And crayons!"

She got this reaction a lot. "Listen, you asked me yesterday how I got the woman who suffered the stroke to regain her hand coordination, to regain part of her life. This is how." She slammed her hand down on top of the coloring book.

The smoldering look on his face told her he wanted to just explode, but he didn't.

"It's a Christmas coloring book, Timothy. She opened the book and flipped through a few pages. "See how finely detailed it is? If you are dedicated, over time you might very well, regain some of the control in your hand and your fingers. I mean, what can it hurt to try? No one's here but us. Nothing leaves these four walls unless you tell someone." She watched as he inhaled and exhaled. "And," she added. "I won't look over your shoulder while you work. I won't look at all if you don't want me to. All I ask is that you try."

It all looked like graffiti to Timothy, something your toddler presented you with from playgroup. He shook his head and wondered how a person could go from performing surgery one day, to...this, a year later.

Meggie kept her word and never made eye contact with him or his chicken scratch for over an hour, until his hand and wrist ached unmercifully. He shook out his hand to try to alleviate the sting, then made an attempt to load the colored pencils back into their box with his left hand. It felt like a bad comedy routine, as he fumbled through what should have been so simple, something he once took for granted. It was just putting pencils back into a box.

"Don't worry about it, Timothy, I'll take care of it."

Her voice was a warm elixir to his ears, and when she took his mangled hand into hers without so much as a cringe, he relaxed. Once again, he admitted, his mother was right. Maybe nothing would come out of the coloring book exercises, but he liked Meggie. As a matter of fact, he found it difficult to get her off his mind since they first met.

"Why don't you move over to the couch and relax for a while?" she suggested. "I have carrot cake from the bakery downstairs." Then she smiled and his heart turned over. Like a foolish school boy experiencing his first crush.

"Relaxing sounds great, and this cake you speak of only sweetens the deal."

As he sunk into her comfy couch, the tension of the day melted away. He took the time look around her apartment. It was even smaller than the one he'd first rented in college. The homey touches—the patchwork quilt draped over the couch, the antique rocking chair, even the little decorated Christmas tree perched on a table and surrounded by Christmas cards—added to the charm.

"So, are you doing anything special for Christmas?" she asked from the kitchen.

*Was this an invitation?* He wondered. *Probably not. She was just making polite conversation.*

"Ah...no. I'll visit my mother, maybe have dinner with her, and that's about it. I'm not much of a Christmas person. What about you?"

She walked into the living room and placed a small china plate, with a fork, and a perfect slice of carrot cake on the table in front of him. "I like Christmas, but..." she paused momentarily. "I'm an only child, and both of my parents passed away. I have a few scattered relatives, but none I'd actually go and visit. I usually go to see a movie Christmas Eve, and another Christmas Day."

It sounded like a worse way to spend Christmas than he envisioned for himself, but he didn't say it out loud. Instead, he asked, "Aren't you going to visit my mother? I know she'd love that." If she did visit, he could see her and then maybe go to that movie with her. Of course, that was just wishful thinking. When Meggie agreed to treat him with her alternative therapy, he felt certain she wasn't looking for a man, or even a date for Christmas.

"Yes, I plan to visit your mother Christmas Eve, so I won't infringe on her family time with you." She sat on the rocker across from him.

"Meggie, my mother thinks of you as family. You can visit Christmas Eve and Christmas, she'd love that. Since she went in to assisted living after her surgery, her life changed radically. She's surrounded by people on a daily basis, and activities galore, but I know she still gets lonely from time to time." As he said the words, he thought of how it echoed his own life.

"Timothy, you look so distant all of a sudden. What's wrong?"

He snapped back to reality. He was about to lie and say 'nothing,' but as he sat there within Meggie's four walls, he wanted to talk about his life, and how it changed, to someone who hopefully didn't have an agenda.

"Talking about my mother just made me think of how much my own life has changed in the last year. One incident changed my life forever."

"What happened?" she asked gently.

"I volunteered a few hours a month at the clinic at the community center. Mostly people who didn't have insurance or the money to see a doctor, came in for everyday ailments—colds, sore throats, vaccinations for children. Basically I was a surgeon who had a dual life every month practicing family medicine."

"How did you like that?"

He stopped to consider her question. "I guess I never gave it much thought, but it was good, I guess…interesting. Babies, kids, geriatrics, pregnant women...It was never the same thing twice." When she didn't comment, he continued. "Anyway, if you're wondering how I got this"—he paused and held up his hand—"there was a fight in the waiting room between two teenage boys over which one was the daddy of some pregnant girl's baby. I didn't know one of them had a knife, and when I tried to break it up, I guess I grabbed for him, and grabbed the knife blade instead. That is where the first cut came from." He stopped and traced the jagged scar on his palm. "The second came when he tried to take the knife back and run away. That's really it, Meg. I was left standing there is a puddle of blood, my career in tatters."

She moved from the rocker and sat beside him on the couch. "I'm so sorry, Timothy."

He waved off her remark as his temper flared. He'd heard it said so many times. "Don't pity me, Meggie. What's happened, happened."

"What's wrong with a little pity, Timothy? Pity means someone cares about you, that they sympathize with what you are going through."

No one ever put things into the exact right words as Meggie did. The right words, and a genuine sense of sincerity. Most people patted his hand, or shook their heads and said, *I'm so sorry*, almost mechanically, or, *There, there, Timothy*, and walked away embarrassed, or at a loss for anything useful to say.

"Meggie, I don't mean to snap at you. I don't want to be like this. You're the first person in the last year who actually makes sense...Who gets me."

When she took his hand again, he found it overwhelmingly comforting. This woman had a gift. "You have the right to feel angry, Timothy. You have the right to feel devastated. Now you have to find how to make yourself happy again."

"Happy? I can't even think of the last time I was genuinely happy," he admitted.

"Well, maybe it's time to change all that. What would make you happy?"

When he looked into her beautiful espresso brown eyes, all he could think to say was, *spending time with you*. If he did, she might bolt, and he'd expose himself as desperate and needy, and that simply could not happen.

"I don't know anymore."

"How about Christmas shopping? Have you bought all your gifts yet?"

Was she kidding? Christmas shopping was the worst. The crowds, with people trampling each other to get the sixty-inch high definition television with surround sound for twenty dollars that the store had exactly one of?

"I'm buying gift cards this year. I can go online and order them, no muss, no fuss."

"No fun!" She laughed. "Christmas shopping doesn't need to be a chore. It can be about getting out among people, and buying things for people you care about."

"So, where do you want your gift card from?" he asked, half-joking and half-serious.

"I don't want a gift card, I want to go shopping. Besides, I know exactly what your mother wants for Christmas, and you're going to surprise her with it—a fuzzy coat she saw at a store in the mall that she says reminds her of a teddy bear."

"Hey, I bought her a very nice tablet computer last year. Ordered it with my right hand, from my hospital bed. She emails me constantly now. Now if that isn't love—"

"And I'm sure your mother appreciates that fact with every email she sends. I'm certain she would appreciate something that you actually chose and wrapped yourself."

He sighed. "You're not going to let this go, are you?"

She smiled.

Oh that smile could do things to him....

"Okay, tomorrow evening, we'll shop," he agreed, not that he planned to say no anyway. Shopping wasn't his first choice, but he felt intrigued by Meggie Marie, and all the little ways she was trying to bring him back to life.

When she let go of his hand and got up from the couch, he felt strangely deflated. She walked to the window and turned back to him. "Come here, Timothy, I want to show you something."

He got up from the couch, quite curious. It was dark outside now, and the main street below was still in full swing. People walked up and down the street. Each store was brightly lit, and gaily decorated in festive colors.

"Look at that, Timothy." She stood so close, he could hear her gentle breath, and feel the heat from her body. "This is Christmas. This is life."

He placed his hand on the icy window. Perhaps it was time to let go of what he couldn't change, and embrace what was still real. If he was strong enough to do it. He stole a glance at Meggie who stared with delight at the hustle and bustle below. Maybe with this woman by his side, he could very well pull himself back from the depths of hell and rejoin the living.

"Alma, I'm sorry, but I can't go on this way. I have to tell Timothy the truth." Meggie was in the middle of dressing for her Christmas shopping trip with Timothy, when Alma phoned for a progress update.

"You can't do that!" Alma protested loudly. "If he finds out I told you everything and was behind orchestrating this little intervention, he'll clam up forever. Besides, you're not lying, you're just withholding the truth...for his sake."

"I'm well aware of that. He'll probably explode when he finds out, and then he'll shut down," Meggie calmly replied. "But, I can't do this, it's against everything I stand for. Lying or withholding the truth, it's all the same to me. Also, give your son more credit. He's finding his way out of the darkness. In the short period of time we've spent together, I can see a marked improvement in his entire attitude. I think it's best to let him find his own way. He's got feel it, Alma."

"Meggie, if he's made any improvement at all, it's because of you. Please don't just walk away now. He'll wonder why, he'll ask questions. You know I'm not a well woman. I don't want to miss seeing my son during whatever time I have left."

She was using guilt now. That was downright nasty and cruel. "He'll find out eventually, Alma, and resent both of us. I'm not family, I'll be fine."

Yet as she said the words, she knew she wouldn't be fine. She liked Timothy. The more she spoke with him, and spent time with him, the more she liked him. If circumstances were different, she could see their relationship blooming beyond a friendship. But not after the way they came together. He would feel betrayed, and never forgive her, and it would probably take a considerable time to forgive his mother. "Listen, Alma. I have to finish getting ready."

"I know, you have a date with my son tonight! He told me. I tell you, Meggie, he is so excited. I haven't heard that in his voice for such a long time."

Suddenly it all became crystal clear to Meggie. This was no secret therapy work his mother coerced her into. Alma was matchmaking!

"Alma, this isn't a date. We're going Christmas shopping. I want Timothy to get out with people again, that's all."

"Of course it is," she replied innocently. "You two go out on the town this evening, and have a great time together. Oh, the nurse is here to take my blood pressure, sweetie. I'll talk to you tomorrow. Bye now!"

Meggie shook her head as she disconnected the call. What a predicament she was caught up in. Now she'd need to figure a way to get everyone out without any hurt feelings or resentment.

Meggie stood in front of the mirror, twisted her hair into a chignon and pinned in a candy cane hairclip to match the red and white dress she wore. For just a

Christmas shopping trip she sure was pulling out all the stops. She was getting in too deep, she knew, as she dabbed on some bright red lip gloss, and finished with a spritz of sugar cookie holiday fragrance.

As she sat on the edge of the couch and waited for Timothy to arrive, she suddenly had an idea that might put an end to all the nonsense and secrecy. He'd taken home the tote bag of coloring books, pencils, markers, and little paper affirmations she placed with sticky notes all through the book. She would simply tell him when he arrived that as long as he continued to keep up with the daily coloring, in time, and with a little luck, some of the dexterity would return to his hand and fingers. It would be sad to end her time with him. Still, in the end, hopefully they all would get out unscathed.

As soon as she opened her door, all the resolve to sever their ties evaporated into the chilly atmosphere when Timothy presented her with a bouquet of the most exquisite roses. They weren't your ordinary garden variety roses, either. In each precious bloom was a rainbow that resembled tie-dye.

"I planned to have them delivered, but I wanted to see the expression on your face when you saw them. You have just surpassed every daydream I've had today."

She stood in the doorway, awestruck. She wasn't sure if it was the roses, his sweet words, or the radiant look on his handsome face.

"They're called *Happy Roses*. When I saw them online, I couldn't help but remember the rose headband, and the tie-dye dress you wore the first day we met at the community center."

"They're beautiful, Timothy. Thank you for being so thoughtful," she said after finally finding her voice. "Come on in, I'm almost ready to go." She backed into her apartment, alternating her focus between Timothy and the roses.

She placed the vase of roses on her kitchen counter, and nearly stumbled in her heels as she groped for her clutch. He caught her as she teetered, and somehow she wound up in his warm embrace, his lips achingly close to hers. She wanted nothing more at that moment than to meld with him, but just as his lips tantalizingly brushed hers, she pulled back and wiggled from his arms.

"Thanks for saving me there." She let out a light chuckle. "I guess we should get going."

Meggie considered their first trip to the mall a resounding success. Yes, it was heaving with Christmas shoppers all looking for that perfect gift that hopefully was on sale as well, and Timothy complained for a good portion of the time, but in the end, they emerged with the teddy bear coat for his mother, and two overpriced chocolate dipped apples rolled in coconut and crushed nuts. Their reward, Timothy proclaimed, for surviving the Christmas explosion of overpriced stuff no one needed to survive—also called the mall—and not being trampled to death in the process.

She loved his wicked sense of humor, and even complaints he found a way to make amusing.

"I'm starving," he moaned, as he loaded the gift into the trunk of the car.

"Well, you didn't want to wait to be seated at any of the restaurants."

"Even if I did, I didn't want to be within range of breathing in someone else's DNA, besides yours, of course"—he paused and flashed a smirk—"from all those tables pushed so close to one another that you can hear every word of everyone's conversations."

"So what do you suggest?" she asked as she fastened her seatbelt.

"Are you up for a meal that is very un-Christmas, and a place to match?"

"I'm intrigued. By all means, take me there."

Timothy introduced her to Indian cuisine, and she became an instant devotee. The place was a mere hole in the wall on a street of shops closed for the day, with the exception of a bar here and there. The wait staff greeted him by name, with kisses, and exuberant handshakes, and Meggie got the impression he used to eat at the establishment quite often. Until his injury and subsequent withdrawal from most of society. Timothy seemed...no, he *was* happy to be back among people he genuinely enjoyed spending time with. Another success.

This brought her a great secret satisfaction. Yet once again, as they said their goodbyes at the restaurant, with promises to soon return, she was assailed by the knowledge that she someday soon needed to tell Timothy the truth about what she was, and how they really came together. No matter what his mother said or how much she protested, Timothy needed to hear the truth.

When he took her home, walked all the metal steps he hated, and checked over her apartment *just to be sure* all was safe, she walked him to the door.

"Good night, Timothy, I had a wonderful evening. Please be sure to give me a call when you get home, so I know you made it back safely." She shivered a bit from the cold December wind.

"We could do this again, you know. We could do this all the time…if you'd like."

Her conscience prompted her hard to tell him the truth right now and that maybe, just maybe, he'd understand. Yet the words failed her. Instead, she looked into his blue eyes as he pulled her close, his lips descending to meet hers. She allowed herself this one pure pleasure. Just as his tongue gently touched hers, she pulled back.

"We…we can't do this, Timothy." She patted his chest and dropped her head so she couldn't see his face.

He lifted her chin and forced her to make eye contact with him.

"Why not, Meggie? We have this connection. I feel it, don't you?"

"Of course I feel it, Timothy," she said through suddenly trembling lips.

"Then what is troubling you, my darling?"

"I'm your therapist of sorts…we can't have a relationship beyond that."

His brow furrowed. "Why not? We're two consenting adults. What happens between us is just between us. The type of therapy you do is alternative— you don't have a license, right? You're not bound by the same rules as I am as a doctor."

"I know, but…" her voice trailed off.

"But what? I know I want to spend as much time getting to know you as possible. In just the short time you've been in my life, I feel more alive than ever.

I'm actually looking forward to Christmas this year—if it means spending it with you."

He was saying everything she hoped for, both professionally and personally. She wanted to make a difference in his life, and it was working! The side effect was, she was falling hard for him, and maybe he with her as well. He was right, there was a connection between them, a very strong and intense one.

"That's so great," she said, her hand still resting on his chest.

"You are so different, so wonderfully unique and fascinating. From the way you dress, to how you talk, how you act. You're the most caring…genuine woman I think I've ever meet. I can't just ignore that. What if I fire you?" he asked.

A chuckle escaped from her lips. When she looked up, she saw a serious expression on his face, and the laugh died in her throat. "Oh, Timothy, are you serious?"

"I am. You're fired. Our professional relationship is now severed. Send me your final bill and I will cut you a check. Now you can think about having a personal relationship with me. I'm not pushing, I'm just asking you to consider it. With that, I say goodnight, Meggie." One again, he kissed her, and this time she didn't pull back, and she didn't resist. When she closed the door behind him, her heart still fluttered. As she undressed, took off her makeup, and got ready for bed in anticipation of Timothy's phone call, she had a radical thought.

What if she never told Timothy about the circumstances of their coming together? Really, who would it hurt by staying quiet? No one, that's who. She could find a way to put that information into an imaginative little box, and store it away some where very deeply in her brain. After all, she had his best interests at heart, and technically she was no longer his 'therapist'. And when she really thought about it, she deserved a little happiness in her life, or at the very least, a Merry Christmas spent with a marvelous man.

The days flew by at a remarkable speed, and Christmas Eve just seem to arrive so quickly. The more time Meggie spent with Timothy, the happier she became. Maybe if soulmates were real, she might have just found hers.

Whether it was just baking peanut butter cookies together at his house, or his strengthening his hand and improving his dexterity by writing out Christmas cards while she addressed the envelopes, to the evenings they spent just kissing on the couch, until her lips were still tingling the next morning. And he colored, how he colored!

Every time they saw each other, he had another page of Christmas coloring for her. With each day that passed, his coloring was just a tiny bit more within the lines, but the progress was undeniable. Yet it was his pride, more than his progress that impressed her the most, and filled her heart with joy and love. When it was right, you just knew it, and she and Timothy were right.

But try as she might, she could not get the way they met out of her mind. The deception she shared with his mother still remained at the forefront of her conscience, and she did her best to avoid Alma, even though it only put off the inevitable. The truth was, she was an honest woman at heart. If she continued to withhold the truth from Timothy, it would eventually singe a part of her soul. Their relationship would always have that little black cloud above them that only she could see. And what if Alma someday had an attack of conscience herself, and came clean to her son? What if, God forbid, it came sometime in the future? Timothy already made it abundantly clear he was a marrying man, and he wanted to be a father. What if they were a happy family when his mother told him everything? It was time to confess all.

Timothy would be by to pick her up from her apartment after she spent a few hours at the assisted living community. She would give Alma the courtesy of letting her know that she was telling Timothy everything, and no matter how much guilting, prodding, or even bullying Alma did, Meggie would not be swayed. By the end of the day, she might lose Timothy and his love forever, but he deserved the truth, and she deserved peace of mind.

The grey skies above reflected her somber mood as she entered the building. She turned on a smile she didn't feel, and hoped it was convincing, as she forced her attention to the little Christmas party the staff put together for the residents. After an hour, she slipped away to Alma's room.

"Everything is coming together just as we planned!" Alma gushed.

"I'm telling Timothy everything today, Alma. It's been killing me keeping it from him all these weeks. I let it go on far too long, and I can't enjoy Christmas while I'm holding back secrets."

"You...you can't do that, Meggie!" She reached for Meggie's hand and grasped it tightly. "If you tell him, it will ruin everything. He'll lash out at both of us. Why ruin what is so nice?"

Meggie shook off her grip. "Because it's wrong, Alma. I should have never agreed to this debacle in the first place. You'll just have to figure out a way to make things right with your son. I'm sorry if this ruins your Christmas, but know that my Christmas, as well as Timothy's, will be ruined as well." Before Alma could wear her down, Meggie grabbed her coat and clutch, wished Alma a Merry Christmas, because after today she doubted the woman would want to see her ever again, and beat a hasty retreat for the exit. As she stepped into the train heaving with people anxious to get home to their loved ones and festivities, she wondered if she should have just splurged on a taxi.

After she got off the train and walked the few blocks to her apartment, she was surprised to see

Timothy waiting for her in his silver sedan. She thought she would have time to decompress for a little while and rehearse what she was going to tell him. But this talk had waited long enough. It was time to get it over with.

He emerged from the car and immediately enveloped her petite body in his powerful embrace. She held on to him with all her might, knowing this might be the last time he held her.

"I've got some great news." He sounded so happy, that she once again almost dropped her resolve to tell him her not-so-happy news. Yet she couldn't go through Christmas putting off what needed to be said.

"Let's go upstairs," she suggested. "You can tell me your news. I can't wait to hear it."

They ascended the metal steps in silence, and she opened the door and turned on the lights. When she turned back, she found herself in his arms, his lips against hers once more.

"So, tell me your news," she mumbled against his lips.

"Well, you remember how we talked about my future in regard to my career? That I was going to have to find a new path that didn't include using a scalpel?" He let go of her and helped her out of her coat.

"I do. Have you made a decision?" She could hear the excitement in her own voice. If this was to all end between them today, she would know that even though she went about things in the wrong way, something very right came of it.

"Yeah, I got a call from a practice. It's actually the same family practice my mother took me to. The doctor who treated me until I was in college, is retiring. So there is an opening in the practice I could buy into.

It would be treating people of all ages, for everyday ailments. It's a busy practice, but I'm assured the hours would be flexible."

She threw her arms around him. "I'm so happy for you, and so proud. What an amazing Christmas gift!"

"Well, nothing is definite, and I want to talk to you about it in depth after the holidays, because it will mean a huge financial commitment. Since we are moving to what I hope is a future together, you need to weigh in on this decision too."

Her entire body sagged at his words. What he said should have elated her, but knowing what was to come was devastating.

"Is there something wrong, Meggie?" When he focused his blue eyes to her brown, he knew she could no longer hide the truth.

"I have to tell you something, Timothy. Something that may very well change how you feel about me."

"Impossible!" he balked, took her by the hand, and led her to the couch. "Meggie, you're absolutely trembling. What's going on?"

As she opened her mouth to speak the words she so desperately needed to say, no words came forth. Maybe she should show him instead. She reached for her clutch, dug through, and found what she was looking for, a cream-colored business card that she handed to Timothy. She watched his expression as he read the card, and blinked a few times before furrowing his brow.

"You're a grief counselor?" he asked.

"Yes."

"What does this mean... for you and me?" He didn't understand, not that she expected him to.

"I've been counseling your mother since her surgery…since your injury. It deeply affected her as well." When he said nothing, she knew she had to continue. "Your mother was absolutely devastated about your injury, and your emotional state afterward. When you found out you wouldn't be able to resume your surgical career, she feared for your future, knowing how much you loved your specialty."

"Oh God." He palmed his forehead. "She told you everything about me, didn't she? Every little thing!"

"She was grieving, Timothy, and she knew you were as well. That's why she told me everything. She thought I could help you. I wanted her to be up front with you all along, to tell her I knew everything, before she sent you to me. Your mother has a way…"

"Of guilting people. I know."

"I finally told her I couldn't go on with things the way they were, and that you needed to know."

"So all the therapy for my hand—the coloring, the cookies, the shopping, writing out Christmas cards, falling in love with you—that was all part of your grief therapy?" He was strangely emotionless, and that scared her more than if he'd screamed and shouted.

"What we have together has nothing to do with my work in a professional capacity. That is why I was glad when you fired me. I was elated. I still knew you deserved the truth. I never expected our relationship to turn so personal. I doubt you did either. It did, and I'm sorry for how we came together, but know I'm not sorry for how I feel about you."

"You know this changes...everything, right? I mean, I feel like a damn fool. I can't be here right now." He got up from the couch and practically bolted to the front door, and grabbed his jacket.

She felt the sting of tears, but blinked them back.

He reached into the pocket of his jacket and removed a small wrapped package and placed it on a table. "This is for you, if you want it. I actually wrapped it myself. I wanted so badly to buy you a ring, but I didn't think you would accept it this fast. I thought, well, there is always Valentine's Day. But, I guess that's not happening either."

The lack of emotion she saw in him was cracking, and her heart broke for him. "I would have accepted your ring, Timothy," she said sincerely, but knew he didn't believe or care anymore. He simply nodded, and walked out of the door, and out of her life.

A part of her wanted to go after him, but she knew he needed time to sort through his emotions. She only hoped when he processed everything, that all he accomplished in such a short period of time would not be wasted.

She opened the gift, more happy that he wrapped it himself than what could ever be inside. She lifted the lid on the little box to find an antique heart-shaped glass perfume pendant. She remembered admiring it in the window of an antique store during their Christmas shop. She lifted the heart into her hand, and the delicate chain wound around her fingers. Now the tears she fought back, fell freely. She opened the tiny cap and the powerful white floral, hypnotic, uplifting scent of single note jasmine filtered the air.

This was going to be the worst Christmas ever. Still, she wasn't about to sit home staring mindlessly at the television all night. She would get up, dry her tears, and do what she did every Christmas Eve.

"I'm so angry with you." He stopped to consider his words before adding, "No, anger doesn't even begin to cover how I feel right now."

"So Meggie told all, did she?" His mother did not drop a stitch of her knitting.

"How could you, Mother? I mean, seriously, behind my back you told a grief counselor all my problems, and then sent me to meet her under the guise of therapy for my hand?"

"It worked, didn't it?"

It infuriated him to no end that his mother either didn't care that she violated something so personal to him, so painful, or she was oblivious to all the problems she'd caused?

"The only thing that worked is I can't ever trust you or Meggie again."

Finally, she looked up. "Meggie wanted nothing to do with this little plan of mine. Because she is so sweet, and such a kind and amazing person, she went against everything she stands for to help you. And it worked! I haven't seen you as happy as I have these past weeks with Meggie in your life, than I can ever remember. This is how you thank me?"

That was the uncomfortable truth. This December had been the most fun, the most therapeutic of not only the last year since his injury, but maybe always.

"Be that as it may, it was all a facade. Meggie isn't the Meggie I thought she was."

His mother snickered, and resumed her knitting. "What is she then, besides the woman who is turning your life around? I told you that you would fall in love with her, and you have."

"It was all lies, Mom. If things happened a different way…" His voice trailed off.

His mother put aside her yarn and needles, folded her hands in her lap, and looked directly at him. "There was no other way, Timothy." Her tone turned grim. "You were becoming a shell of your former self—angry, hostile, and negative. If I didn't step in when I did, I wasn't going to recognize you very soon."

"I would have gotten through it…in my own time," he retorted.

"You can honestly tell me that you don't love Meggie, that she was nothing but a little amusement in your life? That you can walk away from her and know in your heart—in your soul—that you will never regret losing her?"

He certainly wasn't going to agree with her even though everything she said was true—he already regretted his hasty decision concerning Meggie.

"I take it by your silence, that you can't argue with my logic."

Again, he said nothing.

"All right, Timothy, here it is. I was wrong for what I did. I should never have involved Meggie in my plans. Don't be your stubborn self and ruin what you have together! You know you will never find anyone else like her. She is the right woman for you. I knew that as soon as I met her. Don't forgive me, if that's what it takes. I would rather you despise me and never see me again, than not take a chance on a forever love with Meggie. Can you at least agree with me on that much?"

He was still upset, but thinking more clearly now. Although his mother went about things in an entirely wrong way, she did it for the right reasons: to bring Meggie into his life. That was her Christmas gift to him.

*Meggie.*

He had to find her and apologize, beg her if he had to. This Christmas was going to be the best yet, it had to be.

"Mom, I gotta go find Meggie. I'll see you tomorrow for Christmas." He placed a kiss on top of her head. "Thank you for what you did, but please,

please don't go about things the way you did ever again, okay?"

"I won't have to. My mission is accomplished. Go get your girl."

The place was practically empty when Meggie slipped into a seat near the middle of the theatre with her large sugary soda and assorted candy goodness. The place was old, rundown, and somewhat smelly, but that was part of its weird charm that kept her coming back.

A teenage couple sat in the last row making out. A heavyset, swarthy man whose leer she avoided, took a seat near the front. One or two other people filtered in and sat down. For a moment, she imagined all of the families were together tonight to celebrate Christmas

Eve, and in just a few short hours, the wonderful holiday of Christmas.

She almost had it all this year. Love, happiness, contentment. What happened with Timothy was a hard lesson, but if helped him at all, whether by gaining a bit more control of his hand, or seeing the world in a new way, it was worth it. She only hoped his relationship with his mother didn't suffer too much.

She'd felt sure the theatre would show some uplifting old black-and-white, Christmas feel-good story where everyone was happy and madly in love at the finish. Instead, they were showing *Double Indemnity*. Ah well, it would be her company for tonight, and tomorrow, she would be back for *Mildred Pierce*, thus completing another Christmas spent with dead actors spouting lines from the screen.

The lights went down, and the movie began. Meggie was determined to focus on the story before her. As the first hour passed slowly, she found her mind wandering to Timothy—not the horrible last meeting with him where she confessed everything, but the good times. Just shopping at the mall, or baking cookies together, or late night conversations on the telephone, were the happiest she'd been in so long. She would cherish the short time they had together.

Maybe after the New Year, she would pen an apology letter to him. It was doubtful he'd forgive her. No, the deception was too great, but she wanted him to know she was genuinely sorry for her part in the charade.

She heard footsteps slowly walk down the aisle, and stop near the row of seats where she sat. *Please,*

*please keep moving*, she thought to herself. The person bent down close to her ear.

"Is this seat taken?" he asked.

She kept her focus on the screen. "No, you can sit," she answered with all of the tone of speaking to a stranger.

"Thank you," he said, and sat next to her.

Her heart pounded so hard in her chest, she was sure it would burst. He passed a tub of popcorn, and she mechanically picked up a few pieces and popped them into her mouth. She held the straw to her soda to his lips and he took a sip.

"Did I miss anything?" he asked.

"Almost," she replied.

"Am I too late?"

She shook her head. "Just in time, Timothy. Just in time."

The snow was falling heavily when they left the theatre hand in hand. Even though her feet were sticky with who knew what from the filthy theatre floor, and she could still smell a bit of mold and bleach from the old place, she didn't care. They walked the short distance back to her apartment, and up all of the metal steps. She put the key into the lock, and opened the door before turning back. "Are you coming in?" she asked.

"If I'm welcome." His cold fingertips caressed her cheek.

"Of course you're welcome. What I need to know first is if you forgive me." It was at that moment she knew her future...*their* future, rested with his answer.

"There's nothing to forgive, Meggie. I was upset at first, yes, but after my head cleared I realized if I lost you, I would never forgive myself. You are the woman who brought me back to life, who colored my world, and I love you, Meggie. Oh how I love you."

Pure joy bubbled up inside her and she tossed her arms around him. "I love you too, Timothy, always."

"When we cross through the door, Meggie, promise me all the bad things that happened earlier, stay outside. That once we are inside, it's a new beginning for both of us."

She reached up and smoothed back his hair. "I promise, Timothy. I also promise that this coming year will be the best ever for the both of us."

And then they sealed that promise with a kiss, just as the midnight church bells rang out.

"Merry Christmas, Timothy," she whispered as she looked into his handsome face.

"Merry Christmas, my Meggie. Now let's get inside and really start our holiday, and our new life together.

She couldn't agree more.

## *About the Author*
## *Natalie-Nicole Bates*

Her passions in life include books and hockey along with Victorian and Edwardian era photography and antique poison bottles. Natalie contributes her uncharacteristic love of hockey to being born in Russia.

She currently resides in the UK where she is working on her next book and adding to her collection of 19th century post-mortem photos.

Visit Natalie online at www.natalienicolebates.com

You can find more stories such as this at www.bookstogonow.com

If you enjoy this Books to Go Now story please leave a review for the author on Amazon, Goodreads or the site which you purchased the ebook. Thanks!

We pride ourselves with representing great stories at low prices. We want to take you into the digital age offering a market that will allow you to grow along with us in our journey through the new frontier of digital publishing.
Some of our favorite award-winning authors have now joined us. We welcome readers and writers into our community.

We want to make sure that as a reader you are supplied with never-ending great stories. As a company, Books to Go Now, wants its readers and writers supplied with positive experience and encouragement so they will return again and again.

We want to hear from you. Our readers and writers are the cornerstone of our company. If there is something you would like to say or a genre that you would like to see, please email us at inquiry@bookstogonow.com